The Cowboy Next Door

PAUL SHIPTON

Illustrated by Sarah Nayler

.·• dingles&company

First published in the United States of America in 2008 by
dingles & company
P.O. Box 508
Sea Girt, New Jersey 08750

First Printing

Website: www.dingles.com
E-mail: info@dingles.com

Library of Congress Catalog Card Number
2007906301

ISBN
978-1-59646-912-9 (library binding)
978-1-59646-913-6 (paperback)

Printed in China

1

Perkins, the Cowboy

Mrs. Perkins lives next door to us.
One day she was going shopping.

"Can you bring the laundry in?" she
asked Mr. Perkins.

"Yes," he said.

But Mr. Perkins *didn't* bring the
laundry in.

Ten minutes later, we heard a yell
from his house. "YEE-HAH!"

"What's *that*?" asked my sister Jenny.

"There's a cowboy film on TV," I
said. "Mr. Perkins must be watching it."

Soon Mr. Perkins came out into his backyard. He had a cowboy hat on and a kerchief around his neck. He was wearing a pair of big, floppy boots.

"Hello, Mr. Perkins," I called.

Mr. Perkins touched his hat with one finger. "Howdy, Lucas," he said to me. "Howdy, little lady," he said to Jenny.

My sister giggled.

Mr. Perkins took the clothesline and
tied a loop at one end. It was a lasso!

He began to swing it over his head.

"Yee-hah!" cried cowboy
Mr. Perkins.

He threw the loop
toward a tree.

7

But it went past the tree.
It went over the fence.
It went over the bumper of a
passing truck.

Most cowboys would have let go, but
Mr. Perkins was new to being a cowboy.
He *didn't* let go – and he ran all the
way into town.

Mrs. Perkins wasn't happy when she saw the laundry. She wasn't even happy that Mr. Perkins was in the Sunday paper.

It said: "Fastest Cowboy in the West."

2
Perkins, the Pirate

The next week, Mrs. Perkins was going shopping again.

"Can you dig the flowerbeds in the garden?" she asked Mr. Perkins.

"Oh, yes," he said.

But Mr. Perkins *didn't* dig the flowerbeds.

He ran inside.

Chirp

"What's on TV, Lucas?" my sister
asked me.

"A film called *The Treasure of Skull
Island*," I said. "It's about pirates."

Soon Mr. Perkins came out into his garden. He had an eye patch on and his kerchief around his head.

He didn't have a parrot, but he had Mrs Perkins' parakeet on his shoulder. It didn't look very happy.

Mr. Perkins saw me and shouted,
"There's treasure on this island, matey!"
Jenny giggled.

Mr. Perkins looked at a map and
walked around his backyard.

At last, he stopped and began to dig a big hole with his spade.

"Mrs. Perkins won't like that," I said to Jenny.

But then we heard a CLANG! as the spade hit something.

CLANG!

"Gold! I've found gold!" cried pirate Mr. Perkins. He dug faster. But it wasn't gold. It was water – lots of it.

A big jet of water shot into the air.

The parakeet flew off with a squawk, but Mr. Perkins was not so quick. He got very wet.

Mrs. Perkins wasn't very happy
when she saw her flowerbeds.

She wasn't even happy that
Mr. Perkins was in the Sunday paper
again.

It said: "Pirate Hits Water Pipe."

3

Perkins, the King
of the Jungle

The next week, Mrs. Perkins was going shopping again. She looked a little worried.

"Can you do the dishes?" she asked Mr. Perkins.

"Yes!" he said.

"*Just* the dishes?" said Mrs. Perkins.

"Oh, yes!"

But Mr. Perkins *didn't* do the dishes. He went and sat down in front of the TV.

I looked to see what was on. Oh no! There was a film called *King of the Jungle*. It was about a man who lived with the animals in the jungle.

Jenny and I ran into the garden.
We didn't have long to wait.

Soon there was a loud yell.

"AAAAAA-OOOOOO-AAAAAAA-
OOOOOOOOO-AAAAAAAH!"

It was Mr. Perkins
doing a King of
the Jungle cry.

Then he came into the yard.
He had on a pair of spotted swimming
trunks and a towel.
He didn't have
a knife, but he
had a spoon
hanging from
his belt.

"Me Perkins!"
he grunted.

Jenny and I grinned. Mr Perkins was looking at our wading pool. The only thing in it was a blow-up toy crocodile.

Mr. Perkins grabbed a branch of the apple tree and swung over the fence.

The branch snapped and he fell.

"OW!"

He jumped up and ran toward
the pool.

"Me Perkins of the Jungle!" he shouted.

He jumped into the pool and began to
fight the crocodile. Water splashed
everywhere.

At last, Mr. Perkins stood up and beat his chest with his fists.

"Perkins is King of the Jungle!" he yelled.

But suddenly there was a noise – HISSSSSSS!

Mr. Perkins froze.

He looked at the toy crocodile.
How could it make a noise?

   Then the crocodile started
to move.

Jungle Mr. Perkins' eyes were big.
How could it MOVE?

"Er…" said Mr. Perkins.

He had just had an awful idea.
Perhaps it was ALIVE…

HISSSSSSSS!

"No," thought Mr. Perkins, as more air began to rush out of the crocodile.

It *was* a toy, and now it had a hole in it.

The crocodile zoomed off.

HISSSSSS ₅ ₅ ₅

We watched it whizz all around
the paddling pool and over the fence
into the Perkins' garden.

Just then, there was a loud
yell from next door: "OW!"

It was a burglar! He was coming out
of the Perkins' window with their TV!
The toy crocodile had hit him on the
head and knocked him down.

Mrs. Perkins wasn't happy when she saw the police car outside her house. But she changed her mind when she heard all about the burglar. She was even happier when Mr. Perkins was in the Sunday paper.

The next week, Mrs. Perkins was going shopping.

Jenny and I were in the front yard.

"What's on TV?" my sister asked me.

I looked in the paper. "It's a space film called *Robots from Planet X*," I said.

Mr. Perkins had just put on the TV.
Mrs. Perkins stopped at the gate.

She dropped her bags and ran back to the house. "Wait! I'm NOT going shopping today!" she shouted.

About the author

I grew up in Manchester, England, but I have lived all over the place – including the United States for ten years. Now I live in Cambridge, England, with my wife and two daughters.

Like many writers, I daydream a lot. What would it be like to be a pirate? A cowboy? Tarzan? In this story, Mr. Perkins just takes the daydreaming one step further.